The White Dove.

by
CHRISTOPH VON SCHMID

1841

The White Dove.

First Printing, April 1999.
Sixteenth Printing, August 2019.
Seventeenth Printing, October 2020.
Eighteenth Printing, March 2021.

Published and manufactured by Lamplighter Publishing; a division of Lamplighter Ministries, Inc.

Printed at Lamplighter Bindery, Mount Morris, NY.

The Lamplighter Collection is a family collection of rare books from the 17th, 18th and 19th centuries. Each edition is printed in an attractive hard-bound collector's format. For more information, call us at 1-888-A-GOSPEL (1-888-246-7735) or 1-570-585-1314, visit us at *www.lamplighter.net* or write:

Lamplighter Publishing
23 State Street
Mount Morris, NY 14510

Author: Christoph von Schmid
Executive Editor: Mark Hamby
Chief Editor: Deborah Hamby
Copy Editors: Darlene Catlett, Deborah Hamby
Layout and Design: Jillian Phillips
Cover Design: Deborah Hamby

ISBN: 1-58474-013-2
ISBN-13: 978-1-58474-013-1
ArrbSnowWhiteVellum, K900

Contents.

Publisher's note: The rules of punctuation, spelling, and even sentence structure of the 1800s were different than our present-day standards. We have chosen to keep the original format as much as possible, editing only when deemed necessary.

Preface.

It is my privilege to introduce to you another classic by Christoph von Schmid, author of *The Basket of Flowers*. Children of all ages will love this remarkable portrayal of selfless friendship, courage, and sacrifice. Typical of von Schmid tales, it is the unexpected heroine who saves the day, but not before the realities of human struggle and suffering are played out on the stage of life. Depicting a time in which "every man does that which is right in his own eyes," *The White Dove* gives meaning to life and reveals the sovereign protection that envelops those who choose to live for the benefit of others. I think the apostle Paul summarizes this story well when he says, "Let nothing be done through selfish ambition or conceit, but in lowliness of mind let each esteem others better than himself. Look not every man to his own interests, but every man also for the interests of others." (Philippians 2:3-4) *The White Dove*—may it encourage you as you encourage others.

Mark Hamby
John 15:13

Special thanks to Keith and Valerie Beerbower
for sharing this treasure with us.

The White Dove.

Chapter I.

Agnes and her White Dove.

N the old castle of Falkenbourg, on the Rhine, there lived, many years ago, a knight named Theobald, with Othilia his wife. The knight was generous and brave. His powerful protection was extended to all around.

The Countess Othilia distributed around numerous alms.[1] She visited

[1]Money, food, or aid given to the poor.

the sick in the neighbouring villages; and the castle was the unfailing refuge of all who had any injury or had need of succour.[2] In Othilia the poor had a generous friend.

Agnes, the only daughter of this virtuous pair, followed the example of her parents. When only eight years old, her greatest pleasure was to make others happy. No wonder, then, that this good family was loved and respected, and that no person ever caught a glimpse of the high towers of Falkenbourg without a hearty blessing on the good people that dwelt within its walls. The blessing of God seemed to rest, in a visible manner, upon the head of Theobald and his family. Their hands were ever open, yet they never knew want; they were as wealthy as any family in the land.

One bright, hot summer day, the Countess and Agnes took a walk after dinner in the garden, which sloped down the side of the mountain. This

[2]Chiefly British: Help; support; relief; aid; deliverance.

passage to the garden was by a long flight of stone steps, descending from a door in the castle wall. The garden was well stocked with every thing that could please the eye; here were clusters of budding roses, and flowers in all their varieties—long rows of pears with their silver blossoms, and blushing cherries peeping from beneath their dark green leaves.

The mother and daughter stood, for awhile, near a fountain in the middle of the garden, amusing themselves with the play of the water, which shot up its crystal wreaths in the bright beams of the summer sun, and descended in a thousand diamond drops, glittering with all the colours of the rainbow. They seated themselves beneath the shade of an arbour that was closed in with an elegant trellis, and set to work upon a garment that was destined for a poor orphan girl. All was silent and peaceable in the garden. The deep calm was interrupted only by the voice of a linnet[3] that, from the top of the neighbouring tree, mingled, from time to time, its melodious notes with the gentle murmur of the fountain.

Suddenly, something caused a rustling in the midst of the foliage that surrounded them; but the movement was so rapid that they could not know what it was. Both looked around in alarm, and instantly a large hawk, darting down, poised itself on its broad wings at the entrance of the arbour. It remained for some moments suspended in the air, with its broad wings spread out to the winds; but as soon as it perceived that some persons were there, it flew away. Agnes sat there so terrified, that she dared not look around her; she had not courage enough to lift up her eyes to see what had occasioned the noise that she had just heard. Her mother smiled and said to her, "Don't be afraid, Agnes. It is only a poor bird that has fled for safety from the hawk."

Agnes then took courage and looked around her. "Ah! see!" her mother

[3]A small finch; the male has a red breast and forehead.

exclaimed, "it is a dove as white as snow. In its fright it has come and taken refuge behind you."

Othilia took it in her hands, and, looking at Agnes with earnestness, said to her, "This evening I will have it roasted for your supper."

"Roasted!" exclaimed Agnes, with astonishment, and she attempted to seize the dove. "Oh, no, dear mother," she said; "you are not talking seriously. The poor little creature has come to put itself under our protection, and how can you have it killed? See how pretty it is! It is as white as snow, and its feet are red and as bright as coral. Ah! see how its little heart is beating! It looks at me with eyes full of innocence, and their expression seems to say, 'Don't do me any ill!' No, poor little bird! I will not harm you."

"Very well, my dear child!" said her mother tenderly. "I only wished to try you. Take the dove into your chamber, and give it some food. Do not drive away the unhappy who come to seek refuge with us. We must be kind to all that are suffering, and even animals themselves have a right to our compassion."

Agnes had a dove-cage made. The roof was red, and the sides were wooden trellis-work painted green. The dove was placed in it, and she set it in a corner of her chamber. Every day she gave it a good supply of food and fresh water, and from time to time she renewed the sand at the bottom of the cage. The dove soon became accustomed to Agnes, and grew tame and domesticated. Whenever its young mistress opened the door of the pretty cage, the bird would take its flight, and would come and peck from the hand of the child the little grains of wheat that she presented to it. It became no longer necessary to close the door of the cage, as the dove never attempted to fly away.

At daybreak, while Agnes was yet asleep, the dove would come flying and alight on her pillow. It would peck at her until she had risen and given it some food. Agnes complained of it to her mother, and said to her, "I know what I shall do. In the future, I will carefully shut the door of the cage every evening, and then it will be unable to get out in the morning."

"Do no such thing, Agnes," replied her mother. "Learn rather, by its example, to rise at an early hour yourself. Early rising is good for the health, and makes the heart light and joyful. Surely you ought to be ashamed if you arose later than a dove." Agnes obeyed her mother's advice, and always arose early in the morning.

One day Agnes was sitting at an open window, sewing. The window was open, and the dove, which had been picking some crumbs at her feet, suddenly flew out and lighted on the next house. Agnes was alarmed and screamed aloud. Her mother ran to know what was the matter. "Oh, my dove!" said Agnes, pointing to the roof where it perched, and was basking in the sun.

"Call it back," said the mother. Agnes did so, and to her inexpressible delight the dove instantly obeyed the call, and perched on her outstretched hand. While Agnes was thus happy, her mother said, "Be you ever as obedient to me as the dove is to you, and you will make me always as happy as you are now. Will you not make me happy?" Agnes did promise, and kept her word.

Another day, after Agnes had watered her flowers in the garden, she was tired, and sat on the green bank beside her mother, near the fountain. The dove, which was now so tame that it had full liberty to fly where it pleased, came and perched on a stone to drink in the fountain.

"See mother," said Agnes, "how carefully it flies from one moss-covered stone to another; how cautiously it avoids the mud between the stones; how clean the little thing is. White is the most difficult of all the colours to preserve in all its purity, and yet I never perceive the least spot upon the shining feathers of my pretty dove."

"But see how careless Agnes is," said

her mother, pointing to Agnes' white frock. When bringing the water-pot from the fountain, she had not taken good care of her clothes, so that some spots were found on them. She blushed when she saw them, but from that day her mother never had to complain of the slightest soil in Agnes' dress.

On another occasion Agnes had taken a walk, which had given her much pleasure, and when she came back to the castle, the dove immediately flew to meet her and gave very clear signs of its joy for her return.

"All day," said a servant, "it has appeared sorrowful about your absence, and has been seeking for you everywhere. I am astonished that a creature without reason can know its mistress and become so attached to her."

"It is true;" replied Agnes; "it is grateful to me for the few grains of corn or wheat that I give it every day."

"But," said her mother to her, "are you always as grateful? You have enjoyed a great deal of pleasure this day, and have you returned thanks to God for it? Let the conduct of the bird be a reminder to you."

Agnes had not yet indeed even thought of returning thanks to God; but from that time she never retired to rest without pouring forth her most ardent thanks to God for all the joys and favours He had bestowed upon her that day.

"Dear little dove," said Agnes early one morning, as she sat at her work and looked at the bird perched on the edge of the table with its bright, beaming eyes fixed on its mistress, "I have learned many good lessons from you, and I owe you many thanks."

"Oh, but the best is to come," said her mother. "The beautiful white dove is a lovely emblem of innocence. It has no guile and no deceit. Our Redeemer included these qualities in His words, 'Be simple as doves.'[4] Ever aim at that noble simplicity; avoid guile, deceit, and

[4]Matthew 10:16

all sorts of evil. God grant that it may one day be said with truth, 'Agnes is as innocent as a dove.'"

The prayer was heard, for such was the character of Agnes with all who knew her.

Chapter II.

The Widow and her Child.

HE Knight Theobald had returned to his castle from a successful expedition against a band of robbers who had been spreading terror throughout the country. Delighted with the success of his expedition, he sat down to take refreshment, and, with a bowl of soup before him, began to relate to his

family how he had captured many of the robbers. He told how he had handed them over to the law, and dispersed the others so that they could no longer trouble the peace and happiness of the land.

The narrative continued for a long time, as the Countess and Agnes had seated themselves before their spinning wheels and applied themselves to their work while listening to the knight with the greatest attention. It was growing late, and the lighted lamp was burning on the table, when a beautiful woman entered the parlor with an imposing air, but paleness on her cheeks. She was clothed in mourning, with a little girl, also dressed in black, leaning on her arm.

The knight, his wife, and little Agnes arose and saluted their unknown visitor, who said, in a voice interrupted by sobs, "God preserve you, most noble knight! Although I have never seen you before, I come nevertheless for protection. I am Rosalind of Hohenbourg, and this is my

daughter, Emma. You are no doubt acquainted with the affliction with which God has visited my house. My beloved husband, the brave Adalrich, was killed in the bloody battle fought last year. Oh, how much I have lost in him! He was a noble knight, a good and affectionate husband, the best of fathers. You knew him well. He was so good to the poor that he has left us only a slender inheritance; his treasures are stored up in heaven. But behold, two knights, my neighbours, covetous of riches, are violently persecuting me, and they now wish to rob us even of that which is necessary to live. One wishes to seize my corn-fields and pasture-lands, up to the very walls of my castle; the other threatens to rob me of my forests, that come up to my gates at the other side. Since the death of my husband, how much they are changed! Greed has changed my husband's friends into my bitterest enemies.

'Too well my husband foresaw this, and with his last breath he mentioned your name. 'Trust in God,' he said, 'and confide in the Knight Theobald, and no enemy shall hurt you!' Oh, prove to me the truth of these last words of my dying husband. Ah! what will become of me if I should lose all my property, if I have nothing but my castle walls? Can the stones feed Emma and me? If, some day—but may God preserve you from it—you should meet my husband's fate, and your lady and daughter be poor and helpless as we, may they find a strong arm to help them in the hour of need!"

Little Emma, who was about the same age as Agnes, approached Theobald, and with tears in her eyes said to him, "Generous knight, be a father to me, and do not drive me away from you."

Upon hearing such a tender plea, Rosalind crouched to the floor in tears. Theobald, however, preserved a grave and serious demeanour. As he was accustomed to do, he sat in silence supporting his chin upon his hand, with his eyes fixed upon the ground. Agnes said to him, weeping, "My dear father, have pity upon them. See! when my dove, flying from the talons of a bird of prey, came and put itself under my protection, my mother said we must not drive away the unhappy who come to us for protection. She was delighted that I had pity on the poor little creature. And this child and her mother, do not they deserve still more compassion and pity than a dove? Oh, save them from the clutches of these worthless knights."

The knight, who was deeply moved, answered, "Very well, my dear Agnes. With the help of God, I will protect them. My silence was not from hesitation, but I was thinking of the best means of defending this noble lady and her child." The knight rose, and brought a chair for the mother, and little Agnes did the same for the daughter. Othilia left the room, and went to prepare a suitable repast[5] for her unexpected guests; for in those days, the lady of the house attended to the cares of the cookery.

Theobald then asked the grounds of the unreasonable claims of the two knights, and was convinced that Rosalind was deeply injured and concluded by saying, "Madame, as far as I am able to see, your rights are perfectly established. Tomorrow morning at break of day I will set out, accompanied by some knights, to examine into the feasibility of the claims of your foes. As for you, remain here with your child until my return,

[5]Meal.

and you shall soon learn the good news that I hope to return with."

The next morning, the knight and his companions departed.

Agnes was delighted that Emma was to spend some days with her. She conducted her young guest to her chamber and through the garden, and showed her all her wardrobe, her flowers, and her dove.

In a short time they were warm friends; for Emma, too, was a good and well educated girl.

In a few days Theobald returned. "Good news," said he, when he entered the hall. "Your enemies have renounced their claims, and the dispute is at an end. Though I proved clearly that their claims were unjust, they paid very little attention to me; but they took another tone when I told them that the slightest injury done to you would be a declaration of war against me. Have courage and hope, noble lady! No stranger shall reap your fertile fields, nor fell the trees of your paternal forests. Consider yourself as under my protection, and rely upon me at all times."

The lady was overwhelmed with joy, and tears of gratitude rose in her eyes.

"May God, the faithful protector of the widow and orphan," said she, "reward you for the favour you have done to me and my child; may He protect you from all evil, and guard you in the hour of need."

She then prepared to return without delay to Hohenbourg. Agnes and Emma were overwhelmed with grief for their separation. It was then that Agnes remembered to give her young friend some token of remembrance, as was the custom of those days. Emma had often expressed a desire to possess so tame and gentle a dove, so Agnes went to fetch it. She pressed it for a moment against her cheeks, wet with tears; and, notwithstanding her strong attachment to the beautiful bird, she presented it to her friend. At first Emma positively refused to take it, but after a warm contest with her affectionate friend, she consented. Agnes also gave her the pretty cage, and commended the dove to her with all the earnestness of an attentive mother when confiding a child to the hands of strangers.

But Emma was scarcely gone, when Agnes was sorry for having given the dove. "Mother," she said, "it would have been much better, had I given my gold earrings, as a keepsake, to my friend."

But her mother said, "You can do so when she comes again. The present you gave was far more suitable on this occasion. A more costly gift might have been considered humiliating. To present her the thing most dear to you, even though it should be of little value, is a strong proof of your love and friendship. Do not regret what you have done. See, your good father was ready to risk his life to defend an injured lady; and it was very good of you to give your dove, the object of your most cherished delights, that you might afford joy to the sorrowful orphan. Whoever does not learn to sacrifice every earthly good, no matter how dear, for the benefit of his afflicted fellow-creatures, can have no real love for them. Such sacrifices are the noblest that we can offer to God. He will reward you amply for your generous present."

Chapter III.

The Robbers.

ONE evening, as Lady Rosalind and her daughter now lived content and in peace within the walls of her old castle, two strangers knocked at the castle gate and asked for a night's lodging. They were dressed in the usual style of pilgrims[6]—a long dark brown robe, scallop shells in their hats, and

[6]In the Middle Ages, many Christians journeyed, as pilgrims, to the Holy Land.

the pilgrim's staff in their hands. The servant who opened the gate to them, having announced their arrival, was ordered to introduce them into the lower hall, and to serve them with supper. When they had finished their repast, Rosalind herself descended, with Emma, to see them.

The pilgrims told them many tales of the Holy Land, and every one listened with the most lively attention, but none was more deeply interested in the wonderful narratives than little Emma. The tears flowed at each story, and before they were over, she would give the world to visit, even once, that Holy Land, where our Saviour lived and died. It was a pious wish, but her joy was dashed as she feared she could never gratify it.

"Emma, my dear," said her mother, "we are able every hour of the day to visit that country, and see the Mount of Olives and Calvary, as well as the tomb of our Lord. We have only to read the Bible. By it we can accompany Jesus on the waters of Galilee, in the temple at Jerusalem, and upon the mountain where He taught the disciples. We will be able to see Him healing the leper, making the lame to walk and blind to see, and even raising little children from the dead. But most of all, you will see how He lived the life of a servant and was even willing to suffer and die for our sins. If we know Him as our Saviour, then we can profit by the lessons and example of His life. If we suffer, we shall also reign with Him; if we be dead with Him, we shall also live with Him, in a new Holy Land."

The pilgrims then sought for information about the surrounding country, and spoke much with regard to the castle of Falkenbourg. They extolled beyond measure the Knight Theobald. "If his castle was not so far from our way," said the elder of the two, "and we had any hope of finding him at home, we would willingly go out of our way, that we might see him."

Rosalind assured them that the road they were about to take passed near to Falkenbourg; and that the Knight Theobald, who had only just returned to his castle, would now be found at home.

"I am delighted to hear of it," exclaimed the pilgrim. "It will be a great pleasure to meet him at his castle. I have important matters to arrange with him; and tomorrow morning we will set out for Falkenbourg."

After the morning meal, and as the pilgrims were departing, Rosalind and Emma sent kind remembrances to the Knight Theobald, Othilia, and Agnes. Each of the pilgrims had a small piece of money given to them; and Emma very urgently requested them to tell the little Agnes that the white dove was well.

Rosalind had understood, from the words of the pilgrims, that they were not acquainted with the road; so she ordered one of the servant-boys to be ready in the morning early, to conduct them; and then taking her leave, she wished the pilgrims a good night.

Next morning the pilgrims set out.

The young guide was proud of his errand, and insisted on being allowed to carry their wallets.[7] They took no notice of him, but walked on silently. For a while the road was very uneven, up hill and down hill, but at length, having reached the top of a very steep hill, they came on a level road and began to converse in Italian. The servant-boy who accompanied them was also an Italian. Leonard was the name usually given him in the castle, but he was much better pleased to be called Leonardo, as in his native land. He was a poor orphan boy, whom Sir Adalrich, touched with compassion, had taken up and brought with him to Germany. Although the youth had learned to converse in German, he had not yet forgotten the Italian. He listened with delight to the pilgrims, and was just going to say how happy he was to hear once more the sweet sounds of his native tongue, when he suddenly shrunk back, chilled and horrified at

[7]Knapsacks; bags for carrying articles during a journey.

what they were saying. He learned that they were not pilgrims, but that they merely wore the dress as a disguise; that the country they were passing through was not so little known to them as they pretended; that they belonged to that band of robbers which Theobald had punished so severely, and that they were now burning with revenge. They wished, under disguise of the saintly dress, to go to his castle and get a night's lodging; but that at the dead of night, when all was still, they were to rise and massacre Theobald and all his family, then plunder his castle and reduce it to ashes.

As soon as the towers of Falkenbourg appeared in the grey distance, between two wooded mountains, Lupo, the old bandit, said to his younger companion, Orso, "See the dragon-nest of that horrible butcher, who brought so many of our brave boys to the gallows. He shall soon die the death of the tyrant."

"Yes," answered Orso; "still the mission endangers our necks. If it fails, we are dead. But a chance of getting the knight's bags of gold is worth the risk."

"His life," said the old robber, with a revengeful scowl, "his murder would give more joy than his bags of gold, though I have an eye to them, too. Once safe out of this venture, and our fortunes are made, we can retire from trade and live on our money. An idea strikes me just now. What a pleasant thing to dress ourselves in the knight's most splendid robes! You can have his gold collar, and I his knight's cross of precious stones. We will then set out for a far distant land, where no persons will know us. We will give ourselves out for great lords, and we will enjoy in peace the treasures that we shall have captured."

"All that will be very well," replied Orso; "but I know not why this affair causes me much terror and doubt."

"What terror? What doubt?" exclaimed Lupo. "Is not everything well prepared—well understood? Have we not enough accomplices in the country? When three lighted torches shall appear in the window of the chamber occupied by the pilgrims, seven brave and vigorous youths, who have this long time been watching nightly for that signal, will immediately come to our assistance. They can enter by the garden door, which is easy to open from the inside, into the court-yard of the castle. There is one of them who knows all the nooks and chambers and turns as well as his own house. Nine of us will easily overcome the men who are asleep. Take courage then. Success is certain."

Little Leonardo was almost overcome with affright when he heard the details of this horrible plot; but he took care not to let them see that he understood their conversation. He began to walk behind them, gathering flowers and plants, and whistling a tune; but from the bottom of his soul he was praying to the Lord that he would not permit this scheme of the two robbers to succeed. He resolved to accompany them as far as Falkenbourg, and reveal the whole to the Knight Theobald.

While the two robbers were arranging the best means of succeeding, the old robber slipped on a narrow footpath, and had nearly fallen into a deep chasm in the rock. In the fall he was caught by some brambles, and the thorns raising his pilgrim cloak, Leonardo saw under that dark-brown robe, a scarlet doublet[8] and a glittering breastplate of polished steel. A long, sharp dagger was also visible. But the boy acted as if he had not seen them. The old villain suddenly concealed the dagger and pulled down his pilgrim cloak, casting at the same time a hawk's glance at the poor trembling boy. He looked at him again and again, from different aspects, but Leonardo did not flinch. They now came to the brink of a frightful ravine, through which a mountain torrent, swollen with the heavy rains, roared and tumbled beneath them. Two rocks,

[8] A quilted vest reinforced with mail.

covered with bushes, overhung the sides of the gulf; and a long and narrow pine tree that had only been smoothed on one side, joined the two sides and served as a bridge. This was

their only path. As they approached it, the older robber said in Italian, "It is possible that the boy has noticed my arms, and he may suspect us. When he is passing over this bridge, I will give him a push that will send him to the bottom of the abyss. We shall then be perfectly secure—he shall tell no tales."

At these words poor Leonardo was ready to drop with fear. He stood still, some paces before he came to the terrible passage, and cried, "I am afraid; my head is dizzy."

But the older robber said to him, "Don't be afraid, my lad! Come here! I will carry you over to the other bank." He advanced towards the boy, with his arms extended to take hold of him; but Leonardo screamed and fled, and he was already prepared to take flight into the neighbouring wood as soon as the robber should be within a few paces of him.

"Ah!" cried the poor youth, trembling; "let me go; both of us would fall into the flood. And though I got over safe, how could I come back? Let me go back to the castle; you have no more need of a guide. See, there is the road; and the castle of Falkenbourg is not very far off. You cannot miss your way."

The younger robber attributed the

fright of the young guide solely to the sight of the terrible passage, at which he himself shuddered; and he said in Italian to his companion, “Let him go, Lupo, the boy has seen nothing; even if he suspected anything, what does it matter to us? He does not understand our language, and cannot know our projects. Would anyone pay attention to his words? Let the poor scamp run, then.”

“Well, be it so,” replied the other; “but for greater security, we will destroy the bridge. Then, though the fellow should know, he cannot baffle our plans. There is Falkenbourg. There is no bridge or ford over this stream for several leagues at either side of us. It is then impossible for any one to bring news from the other side before our plan will be executed.”

The two bandits then took their wallets from the boy, and left Leonardo free to go back, but without one kind word for having conducted them. When they were on the other side of the torrent, Lupo called out to him, in

German, "My boy, you are right! That was a dangerous passage. The bridge is mossy with age, and is half rotten. One might easily lose one's life here. To prevent any misfortune of that kind, we will destroy it. The people of the country will soon be able to construct a more secure one."

The two robbers detached the beam, and it rolled with a crash to the bottom of the abyss, where the foaming torrent, beating upon it, soon tore it to shivers.

As soon as they had disappeared behind the hill around which the road ascended, Leonardo began to run with all his strength that he might announce the frightful news to his worthy mistress; for he did not know any one in the country to whom he could with safety confide his terrible secret.

Chapter IV.

The Dove's Message.

OSALIND, residing tranquilly in her castle at Hohenbourg, little thought of the danger that menaced her protector, the noble Theobald. Since the departure of the pilgrims, Emma's mind was entirely captivated by their narratives, and she asked her mother a thousand questions about the Holy Land. The day was given to their usual occupations, but at the approach of evening, when the sun was descending, and a refreshing breeze cooled the air, they descended from their mountain castle, to view their lands in the adjacent valley. The crops presented a magnificent appearance, and some fields of wheat, with the golden ears shining in the sun, promised a rich harvest. The mother and daughter felt doubly happy, because they looked upon these fields as a recent present from heaven, and fervently thanked their God for His bounteous favours.

At that time Leonardo came up, covered with perspiration, and almost out of breath. "Oh, my good mistress!" he cried, joining his hands, "I have horrible news to tell. These two men are not pilgrims, but robbers and murderers. They wish to murder the Knight Theobald and all his household, and to rob and burn his castle." The frightened boy could say no more. Quite out of breath, and entirely exhausted, he sank down at the foot of a pear tree that stood by the roadside, and he remained thus a long time before he was able to utter a single word.

Rosalind and Emma were overwhelmed with grief.

"Oh!" exclaimed Rosalind, "what shocking and frightful news this is! Oh, noble knight, generous lady!"

"And my own kind Agnes," said Emma, trembling and pale as death. "Ah! if she and her parents should perish, I should die of grief."

"Run, Emma!" said Rosalind, "go before me. Run to our castle. I will follow you with poor Leonardo as quickly as I can. Run with all your strength, and call our people. Let them mount their horses, and fly to Falkenbourg to inform Theobald of the danger that threatens him. Let them hasten at their uttermost speed. Let them drive, though they were to sink their horses to the earth."

Emma sprung swift as a roe up the steep side of the mountain, and rushing into the castle gate, alarmed all the domestics by her cries. They rushed into the court, and she told them that fire and sword were descending on devoted Falkenbourg. The news fell like a thunderbolt on the whole family; they were all seized with terror, lamenting as much as if they saw their own castle consumed in the flames.

A moment afterwards, Rosalind came up and entered the court-yard with the boy, whom she had questioned on the way and learned all the particulars. "What are you doing there," she exclaimed, "groaning, and with your arms folded? Start—run—save them!"

"It is impossible, my good mistress!" replied the old grey-haired groom. "The two villains have too great a start of us; they are in Falkenbourg already. It is almost evening now, and Falkenbourg is not less than fifteen leagues[9] distant. How could we travel so rapidly in a dark night, over a bad road, torn up now by the winter floods? The best horse in the stable could

[9] A league is approximately three miles.

not bring me to Falkenbourg before daybreak; besides, our farm-horses are bad roadsters, and all the war-horses were sold after your husband's death. There is not in the whole country, far or near, a single horse that could well stand half the journey." The good lady wrung her hands in an agony of grief. She lifted up her eyes to heaven, and tears chased each other down her cheeks. "Oh God," she exclaimed, "there is no help but in Thee. Have pity on the good people who had pity on me! Oh! Emma! Pray to God, my child; pray that He will cause the plot of these villains to fail."

Emma joined her hands, and, with her eyes full of tears, exclaimed, "God of mercy! Come to their assistance, as they came to ours." All those who were then in the court-yard of the castle joined their hands and united their prayers to that of Emma.

"My good men—my brave servants," said Rosalind, "it may be almost impossible to reach Falkenbourg this night, but at least make the attempt.

A few words might save their lives. Ah! if poor Leonardo were not so fatigued with his rapid flight he would set out without delay; but you, Martin," she continued, addressing a young attendant, "you also have good legs. Set out on your way. The foot-path is one-third shorter than the road. I will give you a hundred pieces of gold if you arrive at Falkenbourg in time to be useful."

"It is impossible, my lady," he replied. "Who could find on a dark night the narrow path across the mountains without falling a dozen times down the precipice?"

"Besides," added Leonardo, "the only bridge that there was to pass the torrent is destroyed; and one has need of wings now to cross it."

"Wings!" exclaimed Emma, with joy shining in her eyes. "Now I know how to send a message to Falkenbourg. The Knight Theobald told me to keep my dove carefully shut up for the first few days, for without precaution it would take its flight back again towards the castle; and however distant it may be," she added, "it will certainly find its way back. Let us attach a little note to its neck, and it will very soon be at Falkenbourg."

"Oh, I thank Thee, my God!" exclaimed Rosalind. "Thou hast heard our prayers. Emma, it was the good Lord that inspired you with that thought."

Emma ran to fetch her dove, and Rosalind hastened to write a few lines. She then rolled up the little note, and attached it firmly to the red ribbon that Emma had placed on the dove's neck. Then Emma, accompanied by her mother and all the servants, went out of the castle, and descended into the plain, where they set the dove at liberty to take its flight as it pleased. The dove rose high in the air, where it hovered a few moments, and after sailing two or three times over the castle, took its flight towards Falkenbourg and was soon out of sight.

All the inhabitants of Hohenbourg were delighted at the happy idea of the little girl. They all followed the liberated bird with their eyes and a thousand hearty prayers.

Rosalind and Emma could not avoid feeling acute mental anguish. "Will the dove find the way, and be there in time?" asked the mother. "Oh, if the hawk should pounce on it, or if it fail on the way, or arrive too late, or not be seen and admitted should it reach Falkenbourg, how dreadful are the consequences?"

They both went to the window that looked towards Falkenbourg, and strained their eager eyes over the whole district, praying from the bottom of their hearts. An unspeakable terror froze up all their senses; and they scarcely dared to reflect upon their situation. The shining of a fire in the horizon would inform them that their messenger had not arrived in good time. They never stirred from the window, nor closed their eyes during the night.

Midnight soon came. A stormy and terrible wind howled through the forest, and the sky toward Falkenbourg became dark as pitch. Suddenly, to their great horror, it grew bright. They trembled with fear, and began to pray.

"Oh, mother!" cried Emma, "the flame is rising higher, and still higher! See how the tempestuous wind blows this way!"

They would have fainted, but to their great joy, they soon discovered their error. They saw that it was the full moon, shooting her beams through the murky heavens, and at last rising like a large shield over the summit of the mountain. They remained at the window; but they could not perceive any appearance of a fire in the distance. At length the day dawned, and it was with a lively burst of joy, and with heartfelt thanks to God, that they welcomed the approach, after a terrible night of anguish, of the sweet light of the morning.

Chapter V.

The Guilty Punished.

HE residents of Hohenbourg now felt that the robbers had not succeeded in burning Falkenbourg. Still they were uncertain whether Theobald and his wife and daughter might not have been murdered.

"What would I give to receive good news!" Rosalind frequently exclaimed.

"I would willingly give up all I have in this world." In the meantime, the events that had taken place at Falkenbourg during the night were still a mystery to them; and there remained nothing for them but to wait patiently for news.

The evening before, Theobald, Othilia, and Agnes were sitting round the table with contented hearts and free from all anxiety. The sun was already approaching the horizon. Its brilliant rays shone through the windows, and illuminated the interior of the ancient dining hall. An esquire[10] came to announce the arrival of two pilgrims; and the knight ordered them to be well lodged.

"Take good care of them, and after dinner I will see them myself. Let them come up and give us an account of their pilgrimage. In the mean time, let them have a good dinner."

The esquire left the room. Agnes rejoiced in anticipation of the pleasure she should derive from their conversation.

[10]A youth serving as an attendant or shield-bearer to a medieval knight.

Alas! little did they dream of the frightful catastrophe that hung over them!

As they were sitting happy and contented, Agnes suddenly exclaimed in wonder, "Oh! my little dove." And indeed there it was at the window, with its little wings outspread, and pecking at the glass, as if to ask leave to get in. Agnes opened the window; the dove flew in and perched on her shoulder.

"See what a pretty red ribbon it has round its neck," said Othilia, "and a roll of paper is attached to it. I suppose it is a letter. Children have strange notions sometimes!"

The knight looked at the paper more closely, and saw written on it the words, "Read quickly."

"A pressing message this," said Theobald with a smile. He unrolled the slip of paper, and cast his eyes upon it. Then his countenance changed. "What is this?" he exclaimed, turning pale. "What is the matter?" asked Othilia and her daughter in terror.

Theobald then read—

"Most noble Knight,

The two pilgrims who will present themselves this evening at your castle are robbers. They belong to that gang against which you were lately engaged. The elder is called Lupo, the younger Orso. They have armor and sharp daggers under their pilgrim's dress. This night they intend to murder you and your wife and daughter, to pillage your castle, and then give it up to the flames. They intend then to put on your dress, your knight's uniform, the golden chain and the diamond cross, and thus to deceive others. Seven other villains are lurking in the neighbourhood for the expected signal—three torches exposed in the window of the pilgrims' room—upon which they are to enter the castle and give assistance. The two robbers will open to them the garden door and admit them. God grant that the dove may arrive in good time, and that you may be all saved. I had no other means of sending word to you. Do not forget to send instant news of your preservation to your grateful

Rosalind."

"Oh!" said Othilia, with emotion, "that dove is a messenger from heaven, as it once was to Noah, bringing him the olive-branch. Agnes, let us kneel and thank God, as those pious men that were enclosed in the ark knelt. God saves us in a manner not less miraculous."

Theobald, too, knelt; and clasping his hands and raising his eyes to heaven, devoutly thanked God for this great goodness. He requested Othilia and his daughter to go into another chamber. He then buckled on his armour, and girding on his sword, ordered two of his bravest soldiers to be ready at a word.

The knight then sent word to the pilgrims to come up; and they both entered the chamber with a gentle air and many salutations. Lupo, with a humble look and in a low and respectful tone, thus spoke to Theobald, "Powerful and generous Lord and Knight! We come direct from Hohenbourg; and we bring you a thousand kind remembrances to your family. How happy we feel to see, face to face, the hero who fills the world with his glory—the man who has the constant prayer of the widow and the orphan, and the oppressed, and whom the good Lady Rosalind praises and blesses as her most generous benefactor and glorious protector! Oh! what a noble lady! She treated us in the most princely manner. And her charming daughter, Emma, how good and gracious she is! The poor little angel was bathed in tears at the stories of our pilgrimage in the Holy Land. We could converse for whole hours with you and your beloved family of your friends at Hohenbourg. For the present, we will assure you that the mother and daughter, and that beautiful little dove, too, are as well as you could wish them to be."

Theobald at all times hated flattery, but it roused him now to such a degree that he could scarcely restrain himself. Still he suppressed his anger, and in a solemn but calm tone asked, "Who are you?"

"Poor pilgrims," replied Orso; "we are returning from the Holy Land,

and going back to Thuringia, where we were born."

"Your names?" demanded the knight, raising his voice.

"I am called Herman," said Lupo; "and my young companion that you see is named Burkhart."

"What do you want in my castle?" continued Theobald.

"Nothing but hospitality for one night," they replied, bowing. "Tomorrow morning, at the first crowing of the cock, we shall depart. Oh! how great will be the joy of our mothers, on seeing us again!"

"You lie!" the knight then exclaimed, in a voice of thunder. "You are not called Herman, nor you Burkhart; but you are called Lupo; and you, young robber, you are named Orso. You do not come from the Holy Land. You are not pilgrims, but robbers, assassins! Thuringia is not your country. Germany has not given you birth. It is not hospitality for one night that you come here to seek. You are come here to murder, to pillage, and to burn. But I pay you in your own coin—fire and sword shall be your punishment—aye—do you think your pilgrim dress, your crosses, and your shells deceive me? Servants, take from them the garments that they have no right to wear, and let them show themselves in their own dress. Disarm them, chain them, and throw them into the dungeon."

The servants then seized the robbers and pulled off their pilgrim's garments. They then appeared each armed with coats of mail.

"Oh! horrible hypocrisy!" exclaimed the knight, "to disguise the black murderer's heart under the dress of piety; that crime alone deserves death." The robbers were strongly bound, and immediately cast into the dungeon.

When they were shut up, the younger robber said to his companion, "How could that knight know every thing so well, even to the minutest details? He knows even the conversation that we had on the road, about taking his clothes and passing ourselves as knights. Can it be that the boy understood us and betrayed the plot?"

"If so," answered the old fellow, "he must have flown in through the castle window. I never took my eyes off the castle gate, and not one soul has passed over the drawbridge since we arrived. Most certainly, all this is not natural. The knight must have a compact with the devil."

He then threw himself into a horrible passion, and uttered the most frightful imprecations[11] against the knight. "That cruel Theobald," said he, gnashing his teeth, "is the ruin of us all." In his hardness of heart, Lupo would not see that it was he himself who, by his frightful crimes, had plunged himself into that abyss.

Orso, the younger of the two, on the contrary, began to weep, and to despair, and to address reproaches to his companion. "Oh, that I had not followed your bad example," he said,

[11]Curses; insults.

"you promised me a long and happy life, and what awaits me now but a death of tortures? You told me that our life was not wicked, and that God pardons crime in this, and sometimes even in the next life. But the voice of my own conscience told me a very different tale and told me of a future punishment. Oh! that I had listened to it! What good can all my ill-gotten treasures do for me now? I should have honestly earned my livelihood in felling timber, and then my conscience would have been at peace. How much happier my condition would have been, compared with my present situation! But the hand of the Almighty, who sees and punishes the most secret crimes, is laid heavily upon me, and has cast me into this dark prison. All is finished for me in this world."

In the meantime, by order of Theobald, the servants took measures to seize their companions. As soon as night approached and the stars were glimmering in the sky, they placed three lighted torches in the window of the chamber that had usually been assigned, for the night, to pilgrims and travellers.

The keeper of the gate and seven companions were posted in the courtyard, near the little gate, well armed. There they lay in wait for the robbers. They waited a long time—but no one appeared. The castle clock had tolled midnight. The moon had risen and was now illuminating the battlements[12] of the tower. The servants became restless and discouraged. "Is all our trouble lost?" said they to themselves, "the villains, the moment they see us, will fly and escape through the woods."

"An idea has crossed my mind," said the keeper of the gate, "by which we may attract them here more surely." He immediately ran off; but it was not long before he came back, clothed in one of the dresses of the pilgrims, and wearing one of their hats. "They will not recognise me now," he said. "As for you, conceal yourselves there, behind

[12]Notched parapets built on top of a wall for defense.

that buttress, until they come in." The servants once more waited with patience.

A gentle tap was heard at the gate. The gate-keeper opened it cautiously. One of the robbers passed the threshold, and looked at the porter, whom, in his disguise, he took for one of his companions; he said to him, in a low voice, "Have we arrived in time?"

"Just in time," replied the porter, in the same tone. "Be quiet. Enter all of you."

The seven robbers entered, one after another, in silence, and upon tiptoe. They carried with them pitch torches and other combustibles,[13] and every man had his sword drawn. As soon as the last had entered, the porter shut the door and took the key. He then called out, in a loud voice, "Help, now!"

The watchers immediately ran up, and sprang upon the robbers, each seizing his man. At the same moment, Theobald himself arrived

---

[13] A flammable material.

in the court-yard, armed from head to foot, and attended by a number of followers, bearing blazing torches and glittering swords. The moon just then gave to the night the clearness of the day. The robbers were half dead with fear, and did not even find time to draw their swords. They were easily overpowered and bound with fetters; they were flung into the dungeon, that they might there receive the reward of their crimes.

"Such is the fate of the evil-doer," said the knight; "he who digs a pit for his neighbour falls into it himself."

Chapter VI.

Conclusion.

SHUT up in their castle, Rosalind and Emma were waiting, with the most painful suspense, the arrival of the messenger that they expected from Falkenbourg. Many a time did Emma run up the stone steps of the winding staircase that led to the keeper's tower, that she might see with her own eyes whether the much desired messenger was coming; but she discovered nothing. Noon came, and still no news of any kind had reached them. They then relapsed into a state of the greatest uneasiness, and every hour seemed to them so long that they thought they should not live long enough to see it come to a close.

At last, at the approach of evening, while Emma was still keeping watch at the top of the tower, she saw a carriage, escorted by a number of horsemen, come out of the forest and take the road that led to the castle. She flew at once to her mother, "They are coming!—they are safe!" said she, and both ran to meet their friends.

Sir Theobald, with his wife and daughter, had set out on their journey before sunrise, that they might themselves carry to Rosalind and Emma the good news of their deliverance, and thank them in person. Theobald sprang from his horse when he saw Rosalind and Emma. Othilia and Agnes also descended from the carriage, and all expressed their warmest thanks for the happy escape from destruction. Words cannot give an idea of this meeting, nor of the joy, the gratitude, the emotions, that beamed in the faces of the two happy families as they entered the castle.

The evening was celebrated with all the pomp of a festival. The plot, and its discovery and defeat, were the sole topic of conversation. Leonardo, who waited at table, was obliged to repeat, word for word, the conversation of the robbers, and he did so willingly. When he came to that place where the young robber pleaded so hard that he should not be flung into the precipice, he said, "I wish to appeal to your mercy in behalf of that man—let his punishment be merciful, since he was merciful himself." All applauded this good thought of the boy.

After supper, the Knight Theobald, holding up his silver cup, exclaimed, "To the health of Emma! It is owing to her happy idea of making the dove a messenger that your guests from

Falkenbourg are able, at this moment, to thank her that they are not buried under the burning ruins of their castle."

"No," replied Emma, blushing; "it is to the tender compassion that Agnes testified towards her poor dove, and to the goodness that she gave me a proof of, when she presented it to me. It is to her, then, that the honour returns."

"Praise be to God!" added Rosalind, "who has been so kind as to give us children such as you. Be not, however, too proud, my children; for see the poor Italian orphan Leonardo, who, filled with gratitude and love for his benefactors, hastened to the castle out of breath and almost killed himself with running. We owe him many thanks. He has endured hardness, and been a true soldier."

"In truth," exclaimed the Knight Theobald, "you are right! Come," said he, "I will make you a page, for your generous heart ennobles you, and gives you every right to that title."

"We owe tears of gratitude," said

Othilia, "to the generous, the beneficent Adalrich, the deceased husband of Rosalind, for if, in his goodness, he had not received the poor orphan into his castle, where should we have been today?"

"It is true," replied Rosalind; "your safety, which causes us so much joy that we feel as if we ourselves had escaped from peril, has been paid back one hundredfold today for the kindness that my generous Adalrich showed towards poor Leonardo. But has not Theobald been more generous to me and my orphan daughter? The prompt relief he gave us against our enemies could not go unrewarded. He saved us, and God has saved him. He, the faithful Rewarder of all good actions, has rewarded Othilia and Agnes for their friendship to us. To Him be all praise and glory!"

"Yes," said the knight; "it is to God that we should address now, as always, our first thanksgiving. He has showed Himself good to us, and has employed an innocent dove to work great wonders in our favour. Eternal praises to His name! But we should not be ungrateful to our noble friends. That which my sword could not have done, the young Emma has accomplished by the assistance of her little dove. She has protected my castle from treachery and pillage. She has preserved it from ruin. Thus, we see that God is able to overcome the strength of the mighty through the pure in heart, though weak in stature. For by strength shall no man prevail. And since Emma will some day possess this castle, and since she has, notwithstanding her youth, been able, without the assistance of the sword, to preserve to the throne a powerful fortress, I will, in order to reward her, ask of the Emperor permission to bear in her arm a white dove perched upon a green olive-branch."

Othilia replied, "Your idea is very good, and we must see that it shall be carried out. In the meantime, I have a surprise for my dear Emma."

She made a sign to her daughter, and Agnes left the room. In a few minutes, she returned with the dove. Agnes had brought it to the castle in a little cage, but she had not yet said a word about it to her little friend. The dove immediately flew to Emma and perched upon her hand. In a rapture of delight, she noticed with astonishment that the bird carried a gold olive-branch in its beak.

Othilia then said to her, “Let this olive-branch, the glorious symbol of our safety, be to you, my dear Emma, a little token of our gratitude. It was my mother’s bridal gift to me, and I have always worn it as an ornament for my hair, the only use for which it is suitable. My mother, when she gave it to me, repeated a simple old rhyme, which may very well be applied to the events of which we have just been witnesses:

“In every peril, let this olive be
Emblem of God’s protecting
power to thee Even as to
Noah, in the days of yore,
So let it be, till life shall be no more.’”

The End.

Books by A.L.O.E.

The Battle (Sequel to *The Giant Killer*)
Dashed to Pieces
Escape from the Eagle's Nest
Exiles in Babylon *(Heroes of Faith Series)*
The Giant Killer
The Golden Fleece
The Haunted Room
Hebrew Heroes
Ned Franks: The One-Armed Sailor
The Passage
The Pilgrim's Call
Pride and His Prisoners
Rescued from Egypt *(Heroes of Faith Series)*
The Robbers' Cave
The Shepherd of Bethlehem *(Heroes of Faith Series)*
Triumph over Midian *(Heroes of Faith Series)*
The Wanderer in Africa

A.L.O.E. (1821-1893) was born Charlotte Maria Tucker near Barnet, Middlesex, England. She was the sixth child of her parents and was educated at home. Under the pseudonym A.L.O.E. (A Lady of England), she wrote over 140 books for children, most with an obvious moral, and devoted the proceeds to charity. In 1875, she left England for India and spent the rest of her life there, engaged in missionary work.

Books by Christoph von Schmid

The Basket of Flowers
The Bird's Nest
The Captive
Fire in the Sky
The Inheritance
The Little Lamb
The Lost Ruby
The Painted Fly and Other Stories
Rosa of Linden Castle
Schmid's Tales
The White Dove
Worth More Than Gold

Christoph von Schmid (1768-1854) was born in Bavaria, studied theology, and became an ordained priest in 1791. In 1796 he was placed at the head of a large school, where he began writing stories for children, reading them after school hours as a reward, on condition that the children would write the stories down at home. In 1841, he published a complete edition of his scattered writings in 24 volumes. He is considered the pioneer writer of books for children, and his stories have been translated into at least 24 languages.

Books by Mrs. O.F. Walton

Christie, the King's Servant

Christie's Old Organ

Little Faith

The Lost Clue

My Mates and I

A Peep Behind the Scenes

Saved at Sea

Throw Me Overboard

When You Least Expect It

Winter's Folly

Mrs. O.F. Walton (1849-1939) was born Amy Catherine Deck in Kent, England. Shortly after her marriage to Octavius Frank Walton, the couple moved to Jerusalem, where Octavius ministered in a church on Mount Zion and Amy wrote *A Peep Behind the Scenes.* Her book *Christie's Old Organ* was one of the earliest books in history of both Christian and children's literature to be translated and published in Japan.

Books by Amy Le Feuvre

The Captain's Sword
Hero Prince and the Odd One
Jill's Red Bag
The Locked Cupboard
Me and Nobbles
Probable Sons
A Puzzling Pair
The Secret Bridge
A 'Strordinary Little Maid
Teddy's Button
The Treasure of the Secret Cove
An Unexpected Offer

Amy Le Feuvre (1861-1929) was born in London, England, and grew up in a large family. She was a prolific author of children's books with a strong Christian message. Her book *Teddy's Button* was one of the most popular of all late Victorian children's stories.

Books of the Year

Books of the Year are determined by biblical insights, captivating plots, and life-changing character lessons.

- 2020 – Quicksand: Getting to the Bottom
  – Tested
- 2019 – Peace in War
- 2018 – The Treasure of the Secret Cove
  – The Secret Bridge
- 2017 – Launch the Lifeboat
  – Escape from the Eagle's Nest
- 2016 – A 'Strordinary Little Maid
  – The Locked Cupboard
- 2015 – Joseph's Shield
  – The Haunted Room
- 2014 – Frozen Fire
  – Comfortable Troubles
- 2013 – It's All Real True
  – The King's Gold
- 2012 – Jack the Conqueror
  – Falsely Accused
- 2011 – Wälty and the Great Geyer
  – True to the Last
- 2010 – The Wanderer in Africa
  – The White Gypsy
- 2009 – Sir Malcolm and the Missing Prince
  – Exiles in Babylon
- 2008 – My Mates and I
  – The Shepherd of Bethlehem
- 2007 – The Lost Clue
- 2006 – Ishmael
- 2005 – The Giant Killer
  – The Hidden Hand
- 2004 – The Cross Triumphant
- 2003 – Sir Knight of the Splendid Way
- 2002 – Shipwrecked, But Not Lost
- 2001 – Teddy's Button
- 2000 – The Hedge of Thorns
- 1999 – The Lamplighter
- 1998 – A Peep Behind the Scenes
- 1997 – Titus: A Comrade of the Cross
- 1996 – The Basket of Flowers

Illustrated books

We are delighted to present to you this creative collection with beautiful illustrations for young visual learners. Reinforce character building and stimulate imagination with our Illustrated Collection. To view the complete collection, visit www.lamplighter.net.

Trusty: Tried and True

Written by Mark Hamby, *Really* written by Debbie Hamby
Illustrated by Jennifer Brandon

This adorable adventure is bursting with colorful imagery to heighten a child's imagination and stir creativity. Learn about selfishness, pride, and vanity through the characters of Brawny, Smarty, and Beauty, and be inspired by our hero Trusty, who courageously tries to help. This will surely become a family favorite to be read over and over again!

Teddy's Button, Illustrated

Rewritten by Mark Hamby

Join Teddy in his mischievous adventures as he discovers that you don't win the battle with guns and hate, you win the battle with love, and your greatest enemy is yourself. You will never forget what happens when Teddy enlists in the Lord's army!

Lamplighter Theatre

Lamplighter Theatre helps to fulfill the mission of Lamplighter by bringing redemptive hope to the world through dramatic audio. Forged through the commitment and sacrifice of a dedicated team, Lamplighter Theatre now airs on 1800 radio stations in 29 countries. With the talent of world-renowned actors, writers, directors, music composers, and sound engineers, Lamplighter Theatre creatively brings redemptive hope to broken lives, and compels its listeners to live life skillfully and sacrificially for the benefit of others.

Sir Malcolm and the Missing Prince

2-Disc Audio Drama

Inside the castle walls a battle rages in the heart of a widowed king. His son, the young Prince Hubert, has proven himself to be an unworthy heir to the throne. But a bold intervention by the king's most trusted knight could prove to be the cure. In the remote lands of this vast kingdom, far from the walls of the palace, Hugh will learn that the requirement of kingship is servanthood. *Best for ages 6-11.*

Frozen Fire

2-Disc Audio Drama

The events that lead up to Betty's pivotal decision demonstrate the true meaning of humility, servanthood, and love. Inspired by a true story, Betty must come face to face with a dreaded foe. Facing myriad trials, including abandonment and the death-grip of a terrifying blizzard, her love for her devoted servant trumps all. You will fall in love with Betty, whose loyalty is demonstrated through tremendous courage and sacrifice. *Frozen Fire* will keep you on the edge of your seat! Great for the entire family.

Listen to samples and view entire drama collection at

WWW.LAMPLIGHTER.NET

Best For...

The 'Best For' Collections are designed for those individuals who have seen this fascinating collection of books and wondered which books would be best for their children. We have selected an array of stories for each age group to give you just a taste of what Lamplighter books are all about.

BEST FOR AGES 6-11

- Basil; Or, Honesty and Industry
- Christie's Old Organ
- The Giant Killer
- Helen's Temper
- Jack the Conqueror
- Jessica's First Prayer
- Jill's Red Bag
- Joseph's Shield
- Little Sir Galahad
- Little Threads
- Probable Sons
- Teddy's Button
- The White Dove

BEST FOR AGES 9-14

- The Basket of Flowers
- The Captive
- The Golden Thread
- The Hedge of Thorns
- The Little Lamb
- My Golden Ship
- Hand on the Bridle
- A Peep Behind the Scenes
- Rising to the Top
- The Robbers' Cave
- Rosa of Linden Castle
- Shipwrecked, But Not Lost
- Trapped Beneath the Surface
- The White Knights

BEST FOR AGES 12-99

- The Alabaster Box
- Escape from the Eagle's Nest
- The Haunted Room
- The Hidden Hand
- Ishmael
- The Lamplighter
- The Lost Clue
- Sir Knight of the Splendid Way
- The White Gypsy

THE
LAMPLIGHTER MISSION

Printing books of high quality with an emphasis on character development, biblical insights, artistic design, excellence, and skilled craftsmanship is an integral part of the Lamplighter Mission. Guided by our mission "to make ready a people prepared for the Lord" (Luke 1:17), Lamplighter Publishing and Bindery is strategically engaged by building Christlike character one story at a time. Through the mystery and adventure of Lamplighter stories, the framework of character development is formed and the pursuit of excellence is cultivated. The dominant theme of hope is developed by characters who persevere in adversity, being fully convinced that nothing is impossible with God.

It is the Lamplighter commitment that each book instills moral values through role models that either demonstrate exemplary behavior or suffer the consequences of making wrong choices. A riveting plot, a worthy theme, and endearing characters will motivate readers, both young and old, to adopt a similar moral code by emulating the characters that have now been etched into their awakened conscience.

The goal of Lamplighter Ministries is to cultivate a renaissance of creative excellence that inspires one to know God intimately and proclaim Him passionately. At the Lamplighter Guild, students have the opportunity to work alongside world-class actors, scriptwriters, sound designers, music composers, oil painters, theologians, culinary artists, and other master teachers.

Through these masters, Lamplighter Theatre was established, providing a platform from which Lamplighter books are adapted into classic audio dramas now aired in 29 countries. Lamplighter Ministries stands on the shoulders of those who have built a good foundation. It is our commitment to remain faithful to these high standards and inspire others to do the same and more. In the words of Solomon, "Do you see a man skillful in his work? He will stand before kings; he will not stand before obscure men" (Proverbs 22:29).

For more information about Lamplighter Ministries,
visit www.lamplighter.net
or www.lamplighterguild.com.
To order a free catalog go to
www.lamplighter.net or call toll free
1-888-A-GOSPEL (1-888-246-7735).

A DIVISION OF LAMPLIGHTER MINISTRIES INTERNATIONAL

THE WHITE DOVE.

FLESCH-KINCAID READING LEVEL: 6.2.

BIBLICAL INSIGHTS: PP 18, 23, 24, 28, 30, 32-33, 49, 51, 59, 64, 67, 74, 75, 79, 80.

CHARACTER TRAITS: sacrifice, friendship, experiencing deliverance.

To request a catalog, please contact us:
Phone: 1-888-A-GOSPEL (1-888-246-7735)
or 1-570-585-1314
Email: *mail@lamplighter.net*
or visit our website at *www.lamplighter.net*.

ISBN 978-1-58474-013-1